Frank M. Reed

The American Sphinx

Frank M. Reed

The American Sphinx

ISBN/EAN: 9783337390501

Printed in Europe, USA, Canada, Australia, Japan

Cover: Foto ©Andreas Hilbeck / pixelio.de

More available books at **www.hansebooks.com**

THE

AMERICAN SPHINX.

A

CHOICE, CURIOUS, AND COMPLETE COLLECTION

OF

ENIGMAS, ANAGRAMS, CHARADES, SQUARE WORDS, PICTURE
CHARADES, ILLUSTRATED REBUSES, PROBLEMS, PUZ-
ZLES, CRYPTOGRAPHS, RIDDLES, CONUNDRUMS,
METAGRAMS, ACROSTICS, PICTURE PRO-
BLEMS, TRANSPOSITIONS, Etc., Etc.

WITH TWENTY-SIX ILLUSTRATIONS.

THIS BOOK IS
Entered according to Act of Congress, in the year 1874, by
FRANK M. REED,
In the Office of the Librarian of Congress, at Washington, D. C.

THE AMERICAN SPHINX.

1. Enigma—78 Letters.

8, 24, 50, 66, is a vegetable. and is covered by 71, 41, 46.

60, 12 62, 7, is a soft substance.

68, 57, 76, 5, is nothing, but take 22 from it and it is something.

36, 59, 23, is an animal, but add 43, 52, 73, to it, and it becomes the
stem of a plant which grows in India.

14, 63, 56, 3, is a number, but add 71, 54, 31, 37, to it, and it becomes a
play.

16, 72, 25, 64, 19, is on every farm, but add 6, 70, 37, 37, to it, and every
farm would be without it.

37, 1, 55, 34, 75, is in every house, and is sometimes 20, 13, 49, 69, and
sometimes 44, 15, 11.

2, 35, 65, 51, 53, is what we all have but never see.

27, 48, 78, comes in winter, but add 29, 50, 32, 74, to it, and it becomes
a country.

4, 10, 17, is an animal, but add 28, 49, 33, 26, 45 to it, and it becomes a
man in ancient history.

21, 30, 9, is what we all have, but add 38, 77, 18, 61, to it, and it is
painful.

58, 67, 39, is a tree, but add 47 to it, and it will burn, but add 42, 6, 40,
to that, and it becomes an insect.

The whole is an anticipated event, interesting to all Americans.

2. Anagrams.

a. Our sober pets. e. O, ten cats purr. h. Tenant's lime.
b. Sat round. f. Facing sin in it. i. So poet's harp.
c. Counted in. g. Never, Sal. j. In fact, I got air.
d. Patient line.

3. Charade.

My *first* makes my *second*, and my *whole* is held on my *first* and *second;*
my *first* is worshipped, and my *whole* conduces to worship.

4. Square Word.

Our *first* was a poet both witty and sad ;
Then a painter who for wife an authoress had ;
Our *third* by our *second* was constantly used ;
O'er our *fourth* bent our *first* as he pensively mused.

5. Picture Charade.

6. Decapitation.

Entire, I am a troublesome animal ; behead me and I am a river ;
again behead, and I am of service ; again, and I can witness ; once
again and I am part of a poem.

7. A Menagerie.

From *insects* who can sting at will,
Take head and tail, and you will still
   Have *one* more deadly than the first ;
While if a *bird* you likewise treat,
An oft-told prayer you may repeat,
   Which low from burdened heart hath burst.

An *animal* we next dissect
In the same way, and now expect
   A *goddess* from his side to rise ;
But other *animals* will form
A portion of the human frame,
   Not valued for its giant size.

Next find a *bird*, whose brain could plan
A great cathedral's mighty span,
   And *shell*, whose name can well express
   An adjunct of the palmer's dress ;
And last those *animals* we choose,
Who, headless have no warmth to lose.

8. Scriptural Square Word.

Whole, I am the name of a noted shepherd; behead me and add a final letter, and I become a city of the Moabites; behead the second word and add a final letter, and I become a people distinguished for skill as bowmen; behead the third word, and add a final letter, and I become an animal frequently mentioned in the Bible.

9. Illustrated Rebus.

10. Cross Word Enigma.

My *first* is in man, but not in boy,
My *second* is in elate, but not in joy;
My *third* is in early, but not in late;
My *fourth* is in Sarah, but not in Kate;
My *fifth* is in wheel, but not in band,
My *whole* is a species of low land.

11. Miscellaneous Enigma.

I am composed of 44 letters:
My 22, 11, 30, 31, 19 is the name of an editor.
My 41, 21, 5, 16 is a shelf ornament.
My 8, 3, 4, 39, 5, 43, 14, 10, 42 is one of the Southern States.
My 1, 7, 5, 15 is employment.
My 29, 39, 36, 34, 33 is not bundensome.
My 9, 37, 26, 17, 23, 31 is to vacillate.
My 20, 4, 44, 32, 39, 40, 7, 13, 28 is to buy and sell at fairs.
My 2, 24, 12 is fiery.
My 6, 24, 38 is a tray for carrying brick.
My 18, 35, 19, 20, 14 is a quadruped.
My 25, 43, 5, 27 is an animal that lives in water.
My whole is a part of one of the Ten Commandments.

12. Problem.

Determine, by equations of the second degree, the sides of two dissimilar triangles, each containing an area of 5 acres, each having a perimeter of 200 rods, and each having the rectangle contained by one of its sides and a line 20 rods in length, equal to the rectangle contained by the other two.

13. Illustrated Rebus.

14. Puzzle.

I have five letters. I begin as crooked as an S. My *second* is a nut; my *third* was known from the beginning of letters. These three make a German watering-place, to which I come, and, with my *last*, make suffering. My *whole* is a once great nation. What was it?

15. Biblical Enigma—58 Letters.

12, 6, 30, 51, 9, 27, 1, 15, a king mentioned in Second Chronicles.

41, 23, 54, 55, 40, 58, 57, 3, 42, 38, 18, 31, one of the Seven Churches of Asia.

14, 16, 45, 4, 5, 20, 28, 56, what God wishes us to be.

49, 48, 25, 47, 22, 8 was killed by a nail being driven into his temple.

5, 11, 7, 33 1, 38, one who prophesied the destruction of Jerusalem.

29, 23, 43, 28, 33, 40, 19, boasted himself to be somebody.

35, 2, 34, 26, 16, 19, to whom Paul said, "Thou art a child of the devil."

36, 24, 15, 10, 44, 23, 47, 11, 25, whose mother was a Jewess, and whose father a Greek.

13, 28, 12, 53, 16. 52, 30, 39, 22, is what we know God is.

16, 50, 31, 37, 5, 21, 46, 38, a city of Benjamin.

26 8, 32, 51, 31, 38, is the father of 19, 16, 15, 25, 13, 17.

My *whole* is a verse in Ecclesiastes.

16. Crytograph.

Scxcj hp dvcaw gct ass vcgeto.kj
Lc gam gafc hkr sexcj jknsegc,
Ato ocuavwetd scaxc ncgeto kj
Phhwjwcuj ht wgc jatoj hp wegc.

17. Concealed Names of Flowers and Gems.

a Forever, O serene saint! smile upon me.
b. She left the broccoli lying in a pan of ice water.
c. Dear brother Levi, O let me go with you to the forest!
d. Our cousin Ada is young and charmingly beautiful.
e. Lorenzo palliated his sufferings with opium.
f   The dozen barrels of sugar netted $250.
g. Yes, 'tis true, Lydia; Monday will be my wedding-day.
h. You must get up early, to-morrow, Tom, if you want to go fishing.

18. Charades.

a. My *whole*, who was also my *second*, soon made my *first* like himself.
b. My *second* climbed a tree to pluck my *first* and drank my *whole*,
but failed to quench his thirst.

19. Riddle.

What is it that so often proves
    The basis of your thought?
A thousand things you think of now,
    Will then be all forgot.

It is the prisoner's strongest hope,
    The sinner's greatest dread,
The time when God shall blow the trump,
    And bring to life the dead.

We each have one. 'Twas never seen,
    And no two are the same.
Now, gentle reader, with these hints
    You'll surely tell my name.

20. Anagrams.

a. Ravine near it.
b. Treat five men.
c. Permeable tin.
d. Dress up, Ri.
e. I see a worm.
f. I grant reins.
g. Mag's nation.
h. Stir in temper.
i. None in class.
j. Men find I die.

21. Geographical Rebus.

22. Numerical Enigma.

I am composed of 13 letters:
My 1, 4, 13 is an article of commerce.
My 5, 4, 8 is a conveyance.
My 1, 2, 12 is an agricultural implement.
My 7, 3, 4, 5, 6 is a girl's name.
My 8, 9, 10, 11 is a kind of dance.
  My *whole* is a man's name with which we are all familiar,

23. Alphabetical Arithmetic.

FNW)LWAEO(LRO
  L T R
——————
  RSE
  ROL
——————
  OLO
  OFA
——————
  SE

24. Anagram.

A wrod tifly noksep si kile saplep fo logd ni trucspie fo visler.

25. Literary Enigma—128 Letters.

8, 25, 18, 62, 52, 67, 15, 40, 59, 98, 44, 121, one of Dickens' works.

32, 33, 111, 112, 110, 46, 6, an American poet.

5, 24, 56, 58, 52, 70, 13, a character in " Hamlet."

18 61, 84, 66, 16, 11, 64, 63, a pseudonym of an English novelist.

66, 75, 24, 21, 30, 39, 20, 35, 23, 55, 8, a character in Fielding's "History of a Foundling."

78, 42, 53, 46, 2, 95, 48, 12, 19, 14, 1, 10, 29, 117, the *nom de plume* of an American authoress.

9, 83, 4, 41, 118, 27, an English historian.

68, 72, 24, a character in " Great Expectations.

56, 72, 69, 31, 76, 51, 79, 116, a poem by Longfellow.

101, 107, 60, 57, 106, 102, 83, 22, 47, a distinguished American novelist.

13, 26, 46, 61, 86, 94, 100, 66, 107, 75, 70, 37, 99, 98, a poem by Coleridge.

46, 65, 54, 45, 80, 17, 13, 88, 123, 93, 66, a novel by Smollett.

91, 81, 124, 105, 84, a character in "Dombey & Son."

15, 49, 66, 38, 50, 108, 127, 87, 71, 89, 90, a Greek orator.

11, 16, 43, 73, 104, 112, 113, 92, a work by Dr. Johnson.

85, 76, 111, 109, 119, 59, 103, 46, 113, 122, 128, a distinguished poet and novelist.

28, 58, 28, 27, 14, 15, 12, 48, 5, 74, 57, 56, 47, 114, 58, 25, 62, 32, a title bestowed of King Henry VIII. by Leo X.

117, 125, 66, 76, 115, a French novelist.

96, 70, 75, 85, 69, 112, 88, 87, 42, 11, 21, 112, 27, 72, 126, 127, author of " History of the World."

7, 97, 48, 6, 35, 36, a character in " David Copperfield."

7, 12, 13, 82, 108, 44, 17, 77, 112, 120, 22, 38, 85, a popular poem.

The whole is a stanza from a poem by Shelley.

26. Charade.

Job longed for my *first* to engrave his words,
And Abraham carried my *second*
When taking his son to be sacrificed
Where the angel of God had beckoned.

A king of Judah made use of my *whole*,
Ere putting a roll in the fire,
Destroying, in anger, a prophecy
Which was spoken by Jeremiah.

27. Puzzle.

I am a word of five letters : My *third* is one-tenth of the *fifth*. My *fifth* is one-half of the *first*. My *second* and *fourth* stands for yourself. The *whole* is what I hope you all are.

28. Conundrum.

"Please, ma'am, do you want your sidewalk shovelled?"
Why is this boy like silence?

29. Anagrams—Cities in the United States.

a. Hull; Vine St.
b. Mol bent.
c. To tell Rick.
d. Veer, star.
e. See, all song.
f. Take Sall.
g. I'll-fed chit.
h. Sore grub.
i. Men, go try Mo.
j. Rest, Copt
k. I very small.
l. Queer Matt.

30. Cross Word Enigma.

My *first* is in cold but not in warm :
My *second* is in iron but not in lead ;
My *third* is in black but not in white;
My *fourth* is in flour but not in meal;
My *fifth* is in April but not in May ;
My *sixth* is in ocean but not in shore ;
My *seventh* is in old but not in young.
My *eighth* is in four but not in five ;
My *whole* is one of the Territories of the United States.

31. Problem.

A certain triangular tract of land contains in area 112 acres and 64 perches; and the three sides thereof are in proportion to each other as 18 is to 20 and to 21. What is the true length of each of its three respective sides?

32. Illustrated Rebus.

33. Metagram.

I am composed of four letters, and am a division of the earth.
Change my *first*, I signify a modified sound.
Change it again, I am a synonym of solitary.
Change it again, I am used for sharpening edged tools.
Change it again, I signify departing.
Change it again, I am solid body, shaped as a sugar-loaf.

34. Double Acrostic.

In medicine a valuable plant,
One who believes all Scripture is cant;
Part of a house is now brought in view,
The next has sent grief to not a few.
A drink famed as the Englishman's joy,
A metal often used to destroy;
Here is where knights their prowess display,
This one their orders is bound to obey;
For this there are thanks on every hand,
When my next spreads dryness over the land.
Next rises a curtain of any hue,
A science instructive and pleasing, too;
A well-known plant will this bring to light,
With this weapon birds are won't to fight.
   The initials and finals, two poets, whose lays
   Have gained for each an endless praise.

35. Decapitation.

I am a word of one syllable, and one of the principal necessaries of man's life; behead me, and I am indispensable to all life; behead me again, and I am an act indispensable to animal life.

36. Puzzle.

Make sense of the following letters:

```
C E N S E
E M F O M
S I P E I
S N R C T
A D E N L
R I S E L
Y S A T A
```

37. Enigma.

I am composed of 6 letters :
Cut off my head and I form a portion of this republic.
Drop my two next letters and I am something we did yesterday.
My 5, 6, 4, is a beverage.
My 1, 4, 2, 3, is a point of the compass.
My 3, 4, 2, 5, 1, is an intellectual relish
My 2, 6, 4, is a body of water.
My 2, 4, 3, 1, means to satisfy.
My *whole* is something all are willing to possess.

38. Picture Charade.

SHAKESPEARE'S WIFE.   CELEBRATED NURSE.

39. Conundrums.

a. What is the nearest thing to a cat looking out of a window ?
b. Why are wheat and potatoes like Chinese idols ?
c. Why is chloroform like Mendelssohn ?
d. When is a lady's cheek not a cheek ?
e. Why should a teetotaller refrain from marrying ?

40. Conundrum.

What two geographical young ladies of the United States require the services of a dentist, and why?

41. Word Squares.

I.	II.	III.
Extended, a well-known plant and its fruit.	To emit rays.	A general term for the feathered kind.
Vegetable production.	To relieve.	A conception.
A thrust.	A country.	A quantity of paper.
To penetrate.	To design.	A mistress of a family.

42. Illustrated Rebus.

43. Scriptural Acrostic.

The initials of the following names form a request of the Apostles

A wild man.
A mighty hunter.
The shepherd of God.
The ruler of the half of Jerusalem.
Who broke his neck by a fall?
Who built an ivory house?
Who fought with an oxgoad?
Who used a pulpit made of wood?
Who slept on an iron bedstead?
Who was slain for touching the ark?
What rock kept six hundred men?
A governor of Judea.
Who was as light of foot as a wild roe?
Whose spear-head weighed six hundred shekels of brass?
What king made presents to David?
At whose request did the shadow on the dial turn back?

44. Buried Cities.

a. I shot the fox for Dan.

b. During the gale Nate was hurt.

c. Do not nap lest they catch you.

d. The dove rose up and flew.

e. Did Hetty receive an answer ?

f. They encamped in a valley.

g. He got the best one of all.

h. Tell him what Roy said.

45. Biographical Enigma.

I am composed of 85 letters :

My 46, 13, 2, 5, 73, 25, 46, 4, 14, 34, 22, 3, 16, 44, 42, 43, 41, 8, 14, 22, 50 was a celebrated English poet.

My 1, 53, 56, 26, 20, 58, 10, 68, 17, 41, 65, 65, 61, 12, 79, 68 is a famous minister in New York.

My 84, 21, 21, 15, 34, 84, 56, 37, 44, 47, 6, 7, 58, 49, 5, 17, 19 is an American novelist.

My 9, 29, 33, 38, 9, 85, 14, 56 is noted for her lively sketches.

My 78, 55, 37, 24, 18, 60 was a Persian queen.

My 37, 67, 61, 14, 55, 23, 85, 37 was an Anthenian philosopher.

My 73, 68, 39, 45, 27 was one of the nominees for president.

My 37, 29, 68, 29, 28, 37, 78, 57, 57, 67, 45, 37 was an English actress.

My 21, 77, 54, 31, 44, 56 was an English poet.

My 31, 32, 74, 38, 35, 37, 38, 74, 74, 68, 84 was a distinguished Irish poet.

My 52, 74, 68, 39, 61, 79, 76, 68, 42, 42, 66, 86 was an editor in New York City.

My 68, 67, 37, 55, 41, 74, 45, 59, 42, 47, 68 is a French artist.

My 55, 66, 77, 61, 13, 61, 55, 5, 66, 40 was an American poetess.

My 50, 65, 54, 54, 46, 58, 72, 45, 45, was a favorite of King Charles the Second.

My 48, 74, 48, 79 was an English poet.

My 5, 4, 41, 42, 68, 51, 41, 47, 68, 56, 37 was a Scotch poet.

My 62, 74, 38, 79, 68 was a Grecian poet.

My 63, 58, 65, 65, 69 was a member of the Tammany ring.

My 70, 64, 67, 38, 55, 37, 71, 74, 74, 75 was the author of " The Song of the Shirt."

My 81, 55, 68, 68, 78, 79, 80, 41, 65, 65, 61, 83, 65, 5, 37, 82, 74, 58, 25 is an American authoress.

My *whole* is a Bible command.

46. Syncopation.

Syncopate a halter, and get part of the face ; neat, and get a tribe ; a vision and get a measure ; a fashion, and get reputation.

47. Arithmetical Puzzle.

Express exactly one hundred with four figure nines.

48. A Literary Enigma, taken from Longfellow's Works —113 Letters.

52, 19, 14, 22, 42, 113, 60, 2, a village spoken of in "Evangeline."

18, 9, 70, 25, 88, 37, 46, 81, 27, 69, one of his earlier poems.

47, 95, 108, 64, 68, 98, translated from the French.

33, 79, 46, 72, 89, 75, 64, 58, 38, 23, 65, 92, 64, 99, 52, 55, 71, 29, 84, 106, 90, on whose tomb the birds were feasted.

57, 105, 43, 41, 87. 8, 102, 104, 49, 73, 13, 56, 80, 34, 87, 28, a character in the "Golden Legend."

87, 30, 19, 112, 66, 82, 50, 85, 40, 75, 37, 96, 26, 51, is what "he" said.

16, 98, 77, 63, 21, 94, a king who bequeathed his drinking-horn to the monks of Croyland.

111, 69, 91, 102, 67, 50, 74, 58, a character in the "Spanish Student"

25, 45, 4, 57, 76, 39, 54, 17, 107, 12, 112, 110, a character in the "Hiawatha."

6, 78, 62, 61, 25, 31, 44, 98, 5, 83, 53, 3, 59, 109, 11, 100, 15, a poem.

87, 36, 50, 10, 43, 86, 10, 93, 97, "he the sweetest of musicians."

28, 98, 80, 52, 58, 1, 79, 103, the hero of one of the "Tales of a Wayside Inn."

32, 83, 4, 60, 101, 48, 73, 51, 109, 20, 24, 35, 40, 100, 23, 98, 61, 7, a name mentioned in "The Courtship of Miles Standish."

The *whole* is a quotation from "The Courtship of Miles Standish."

49. Illustrated Proverb.

50. Equivocal Words.

a. To entrust—to send to jail—to perform an act.
b. A sort of dictionary—an agreement,
c. Part of a bird—the harvest—to cut the hair.
d. A bird—a bird's song—an implement.
e: A suggestion—a clew—a braid of hair—a sporting implement.
f. A shell-fish—a weed.
g. A tender relation—a bank—as a prefix it impairs age, depopulates a nation, and denaturalizes "his mother's hope."

51. Numerical Enigma.

I am composed of 43 letters:
    My 10, 35, 8, 19, 17, 5, 13, 36, 41 is a small mass of falling ice.
    My 4, 7, 9, 16, 11, 31, 14, 40, 8, 39, 27 is one of the twelve signs.
    My 20, 25, 3, 24, 34, 32, 12 is one who sharpens tools.
    My 2, 21, 30, 26 is an animal.
    My 37, 12, 8, 42, 38, 32, 6 is a table or bench.
    My 28, 29, 33, 43 is an army.   •
    My 23, 1, 26, 18, 15, 22 is constant..
My *whole* is a proverb worth remembering.

52. Do You Know Me?

I was with Adam in Paradise before the fall, but as far as possible, avoided his wife Eve. When they were expelled from the seat of innocence and happiness, I remained behind for ages in the garden of Eden. I took the lead in their punishment for disobedience, and was first in their deliverance. Also I was with the Israelites during their Exodus into the Wilderness. I attended David while he was a shepherd and when on his throne; but was a stranger to Goliath, King Solomon and all his glory. I was once in Chaldea, but had no connection with astrologers, soothsayers, magicians, sorcerers, nor Egyptians. History records no kingdom in the East where I have not been, though I never visited any of their cities. I have since been in Denmark, Holland, Sweden, Poland, Finland, Lapland, England, Scotland, and Ireland, but did not enter into the mountainous principalities of Wales. I was always to be found with children, but shunned the society of men and woman. No lady refuses me entrance into her *boudoir*, though she will not allow me admittance to her sleeping-room. Without my aid she may be comely but not handsome, coy but not modest, polite but not delicate. Without me the fair sex would not find delight, though I myself was never in a joyful state. I shall never enter your home, but when you lie upon your death-bed, I shall be with you from first to last, though I shall not follow you to the grave.

53. Pi.

Rou prenautiot spended lyregat noup eth hecoic fo oru napinmosco.

54. Picture Charade.

55. Cross Word.

My *first* is in draw but not in haul,
My *next* is in short but not in tall;
My *third* is in strong but not in weak;
My *fourth* is in find but not in seek;
My *fifth* is in blanket but not in sheet;
My *sixth* is in bitter but not in sweet;
My *seventh* is in friend but not in foe;
My *eighth* is in come but not in go;
My *whole* is a graceful plant, I ween,
On the cottage porch 'tis often seen.

56. Hour-Glass Puzzle.

The centre letters, read downwards, name a city in the State of New York.

a. Divided.   *d.* A pronoun.   *g.* A flower.
b. A demagogue.   *e.* A vowel.   *h.* To change.
e. A relative.   *f.* A serpent.   *i.* Homage.

57. Biblical Enigma—83 Letters.

32, 3, 12 38, 78, 40, 51, 18, 6, 66, 25, 44, 82, 35, 39, 37, 47, 40, 76, 10, 2, 69, 29, 11, 21, 75, 27, 64, 46, 5, 15, 43, 54, 49, 14, 26, 28, 31, 52, 50, 9, 17, 10, 34, 8, 64, 82, 43, 72, 48, 21, is a verse in Proverbs, re-respecting strong drink.

51, 30, 41, 41, 9, 19, 79, 3, 89, 42, 56, 6, 65, 69, 40, 9, 80, 22, 28, 83, 53, 15, 43, 44, 45. 12, 5, 7, 63, 61, 59, 83, 51, 26, 10, 62, 73, 20, 78, 25, 81, 14, 35, 37, 82, 40, 9, 69, 30, 79, 39, 60, 68, 8, 60, 72, 77, is a verse in Proverbs, respecting prudence of speech.

2, 58, 14, 9, 20, 45, 33, 29, 19, 27, 6, 1, 54, 17, 15, 26, 31, 57, 61, 44, 45, 37, 46, 41, 52. 16, 34, 60, 22, 23, 24, 37, 39 41, 45, 61, 23, 41, 41, 72, 77, 36, 5, 40, 9, 44, 56, 60, 59, 55, 8, 53, 72, is a verse in Proverbs, respecting the reward of good and evil.

8, 18, 41, 30, 79, 69, 15, 28, 7, 73, 21, 25, 45, 33, 26, 48, 35, 4, 51, 68, 5, 70, 7, 42, 32, 3, 13, 44, 19, 49, 23, 57, 76, 11, 58, 41, 45, 71, 68, 41, 60, 43, 67, 74, 12 63, 21, 19, 55, 5, 64, 23, 62, 42, is a verse in Proverbs, respecting forbearance.

The *whole* is a verse in Proverbs.

58. Rebus.

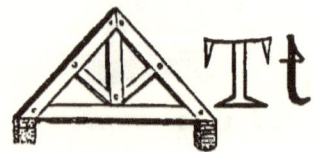

59. Characteristic Initials.

a. Wit Meets Tenderness.   *c.* Hushed Greatness.   *e.* Notes, Words.
b. England's Bright Bard.   *d.* Opposed Cavaliers.   *f.* Weird Concoctor.

60. Cryptograph Charade.

Vh orabc rb cqn wjvn xo j yxnc
Fqxbn vxccx fjb jcfjhb vh bnlxwm
Vh fqxum, cqn orwnbc xo ujwpdjpn rb aultxwnm !

61. Picture Proverb.

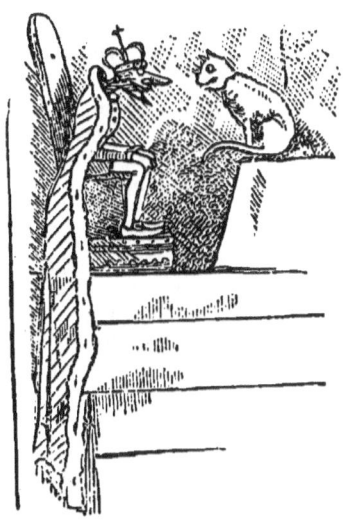

62. Anagrams.

a. Defy it in gin.
b. A moment's cure.
c. I trust a lace.
d. Ripen trees.

e. Cod is nice.
f. I drag a lot.
g. Pat gunner.

h. Salve ruin.
i. I scatche it.
j. Held to corks.

63. Puzzle.

Find a word of six letters, a verb; subtract one letter and leave a verb; subtract another and leave a verb; subtract another and leave a verb; another and leave an adverb; another and leave a pronoun.

64. Charade.

I am composed of two syllables. My *first* is a small animal; behead it, and it becomes a very large animal. My *second* is something often necessary to our bodily comfort; behead it, and it becomes necessary to our soul's content. My *whole* is a well-known flower.

65. Charade.

My *first*, before his head lay low
Beneath the weapon of his foe,
   Was brought into existence
By a word; and by a blow
Decapitated, his sad doom
Was always to exist in gloom,
   And shadowy consistence
Commanded to assume.

My *next*, before it was curtailed,
Full many a traveller regaled,
   And from my *whole* relieving
A refuge safe displayed.
   My *third* is but a form of air,
   But terrible as all declare;
When in the gloom revealing
   His form, all may despair.

My *whole*, of European birth,
Is an artist of undoubted worth,
   Styled by a connoisseur
Queen-songstress of the earth.
But some, who've crossed the sea, recite
My *whole* is but a cause of fright,
   Most awful to endure
And dreadful to the sight.

66. Double Acrostic.

Not all clear; boiling up; a drop of the "crater;" sufficient; too much; part of a house; a musical phrase; a district; gin. The initials read downward, and the finals read upward, will give two wonderful inventions in constant use in the present day.

67. Algebraical Problem.

A set out from C to travel to D at the same time that B left D for C, the distance being 420 miles. When they met, it appeared that A had travelled just as many miles more than B as they travelled hours before meeting. and A arrived at D 35 hours before B got to C. Required—the hourly speed of each.

68. Problem.

Henry, five years ago, invested some money in some profitable business, which yielded unto him yearly one-third of its stock profit; but of which gained profit he spent yearly a certain sum (alike each year). The remainder of that increase, together with the former stock, he yearly invested again in the same business, as a new stock, and with the same ratio of increase, spending sum and result. Now, at the end said five years, it is found that he now has $1.718.20 less than if he had spent nothing of his increase. The question is, what was the original capital?

69. Scriptural Enigma.

I am composed of 49 letters:

My 40, 17, 28, 15, 12, 38 is a mount, a Sabbath day's journey from Jerusalem.

My 31, 24, 20, 33, 3 is one who sought to purchase certain power of the apostles with money.

My 8, 41, 34, 45, 47, 17, 10, 22, 49 was a centurion of the Italian band.

My 35, 4, 21, 26, 23, 31 is a book of the New Testament.

My 44, 37, 29, 17, 17, 19, 49 was an eloquent Jew, born at Alexandria.

My 13, 2, 43, 7, 5, 48, 16, 36, 31 is a silversmith spoken of in the Acts of the Apostles.

My 1, 9, 34, 30, 28, 32, 14 was the person who went with King Agrippa to Cæsarea to salute Festus.

My 6, 26, 11, 28, 42 is a king spoken of in the Acts of the Apostles.

My 39, 48, 44, 18, 14 is something spoken of in the first chapter of Ephesians and second verse that some of us have not got.

My 44, 25, 27, 31 is a book of the New Testament.

My 46, 7, 1, 29 is one of the principal mountains passed by the Israelites in journeying to Canaan.

My *whole* is the language of St. Paul to the Corinthians.

70. Miscellaneous Enigma.

I am composed of 14 letters:

My 1, 7, 11, 5, 1, 14, 11 is a place of amusement.

My 12, 5, 4, 6 is an important article of house use.

My 9, 14, 9, 12, 7 is a numerous race of people.

My 13, 5, 3, 4, 11 is a post town in Michigan.

My 5, 3, 14, 2, 8, 8, 5 was a noted king of ancient times.

My 3, 5, 10, 10, 12 is an article kept by druggists.

My *whole* was a king of ancient times.

71. Geographical Puzzle.

I was going on a journey, so I went out to prepare for it. First I purchased a piece of a city of Russia for an outside wrap, and a city on the Rhine for its perfume. I asked the clerk for my bill, and he said the sum was a division of Africa. I passed on, and soon met a city of Belgium looking for some fowls of a city of France, which he had seen flying through a river of England; but could not see to throw a small range of the Alleghany Mountains, because the river of England was so full of another small portion of the Alleghanies. I went into another store and asked an island of the Irish Sea if he had any silk of the color of a river in Mississippi, of which I bought enough for a dress, and a mount in Oregon to top off with. I then went back to my city in Germany, and began packing my provisions. My box was made of a river of Iowa to keep its contents from a city of the German Empire. I filled it with a piece of a city of New York, a harbor of New Jersey, a lake of Colorado, a group of islands of Oceanica, a river of Vermont, and a city on an island east of Africa. I told a city of Thibet to do up a city of China, and see if the box was full. It was full, and just then I heard a lake of Ireland at the door, and found that a river of South America was holding my horse for me. I took a city of France, which was in full bloom, for a friend, and departed, after receiving a point of Greenland from all my friends.

72. Illustrated Proverb.

73. Anagram.

Thaw rea hhttgsou! a dnwi-pewst mwodea
Gnmmcikii a tredublo aes,
Rea tno fiel dan detah a sodwah,
Morf het kroc ttynreei.

74. Rhyming Answers.

This, being a novelty, requires explanation. Each line of the riddle has its own separate answer, and *all* the answers must rhyme with each other, and not with the ends of the lines. The art is to so blend the lines that they seem to refer to one thing all the way through, when really they have no connection with each other. Here is a very simple example :

> I come from Ireland every day,
> Though on your head I'm glad to stay ;
> Beware my scratch though soft my paw,
> And lay me flat before your door.

Answers : Pat, hat, cat, mat.

Now, boys and girls, here are some that you and your grown-up friends may guess. You will know by their number of lines that I. has eight rhyming answers, II. has four, III. has eight.

I.

> A graceless wretch am I; but see
> How many homes are cheered by me !
> I make you laugh in Dickens' page,
> Yet torture folks of every age.
> Forlorn I wander night and day,
> Most dreaded while the sun's away ;
> Though oft, in peaceful workshops found,
> I shelter men on slaughter bound.

II.

> I'm twice as great as any other ;
> I'm all that's left where men have toiled ;
> I'm never liked, though often borrowed ;
> I'm often born when eggs are boiled.

III.

> Four legs have I, when seen complete,
> And many tongues, yet never eat ;
> Full many a beast I cause to speak,
> And fiery steeds in me are meek ;
> Since my own brother struck me dead,
> I'm pointed out as overhead ;
> I bind the continents together,
> And wear my furs in every weather.

75. Rebus–A Celebrated Roman.

76. Puzzle.

A
NEPI ta PHON
aw OMA nw HOS ol
Dear THEN war EBEN eath
T
HIS St. O! NELIE skath ARIN
e. g RAYC Hanged F ROMA
BUS Y LIF eto LIF el ess C
Lay Bye a R T Hand--c
Lay S Heg! O!! T!!! herp?
ELF, An D No. WS he
St. Urn D Toe Art h. h.
Erselfy Ewe Epi N. G.
Fri END slet MEAD
VI
SE abat Eyo URGR.　IEFA
N DD Ryy ou Rey Es.　FO
R wha!　Ta Vai Lsaf
LOOD
Oft ears W hok N ows BU
Tinar Un O fye! AR sin
SO metal LPIT chero RBRO
AD
Pa NSH einh ERSHOPMAY
Be AGA in.

77. Geographical Enigma.

Find an island belonging to the United States that contains the follow-ing :

1. A river in Switzerland.
2, 3. Two rivers in Asia.
4-9. Six rivers in Germany.
10. A river in Africa.
11-13. Three rivers in England.
14, 15. Two rivers in Scotland.
16. A river in Turkey.
17. A river in Louisiana.
18. A river in North Carolina.
19. A river in Virginia.
20. A lake in Asia.

21. A lake in Turkey.
22. A lake in Africa.
23. A lake in British America.
24. A town in France.
25, 26. Two rivers in Greece.
27, 28. Two towns in Arabia.
29. A town in Afghanistan.
30. A town in the Burmese Empire.
31. A town in Alabama.
32. A town in Georgia.

78. Charade.

My *first* the prairie and the forest treads ;
The daring hunter oft his anger dreads.
My *second* falls before the farmer's men ;
Though crushed to powder, it shall rise again.
My *third* are light or heavy, dark or bright,
And are to mice and children a delight.
My *whole* the farmers prize in winter's cold,
For sweetness is between their folds enrolled ;
And when the grasses spring and blossoms clover,
The farmers sigh because their season's over.

79. Zoological Acrostic.

The initials name a bird of the Parrot family, the finals a bird of the Jay family.

a. A quadruped of the Lemur family.
b. A reptile of the Crocodile family.
c. A quadruped of the Hare family.
d. A bird of the Parrot family.
e. A small fish.
f A large fish.

80. Scriptural Enigma—32 Letters.

32, 4, 3, 18, 12, 6, 28, 13, 4, 15, a lake on which Christ preached.
20, 7, 19, 9, 31, a god of the Philistines.
28, 23, 20, 16, 12, 1, a disciple.
8, 7, 10, 4, 20, 17, 3, 22, 7, an extensive country of Greece.
8, 2, 21, 30. 28, 8, a sister of Aaron.
14, 25, 23, 7, 5, a mount on which God stood.
11, 30, 3, 29, 26, a book in the Old Testament.
4, 24, 27, 9, 18, a place to which the ark of God was sent.
The *whole* is a proverb of Solomon.

81. Rebus.

82. Transposition.

Transpose to color, into a wine measure ; unearthly, into more extensive,—again into a term used in croquet ; a fruit, into a measure of length ; a European river into a bird.

83. Square Word.

A vegetable. To relieve from pain. A continent. Very clean or tidy.

84. Characteristic Initials.

Simple example : Alas ! Beheaded.—Anne Boleyn.

a. Came Confidently
b. Damaged Bears.
c. Ask Liberty.
d. How Worships Booklyn !
e. Lives Not.

f. Several Fine, Brisk Messages.
g. Unless Smoking, Glum.
h. Cannot Die.
i. Her books Sell.

85. Birds Enigmatically Expressed.

a A royal angler.
b. An iron lever.
c. Two are able.

d. A colored letter.
e. A man of war in a hurricane.
f. A field flower with a changed head.

86. Illustrated Proverb.

87. Problem.

A gentleman being asked the time of day, replied that, if to three-fourths of the time from now till midnight you add five-eighths of the time past noon, you will have the time of day. Required, the time of day.

88. Riddle.

I am composed of 4 letters:
Omit my *first*, and I belong to the present.
Cut off my *second*, and I am an exclamation.
Expunge my *third*, and I am at the beginning of winter.
My 1, 3, 2 is a relative.
My 4, 3, 2 signifies success.
My 3, 4, 2 expresses exclusive right.
My *whole* is often to be seen at this time.

89. Buried Cities.

a. He received a sabre stroke on his left arm.
b. Barnstable, on Cape Cod Bay, is noted for fisheries.
c. It was either Æsop or Tom that did the mischief.
d. Jacob lent Zena one of his books.
e. He stayed at Senegran a day and a half.
f. He was an expert hand in the use of the rifle.
g. He hesitated, but Cherbo urged him onward.
h. It happened October 19th.

90. Cross Word.

My *first* is in mountain, but not in hill ;
My *second* in beak, but not in bill.
My *third* in cash, but not in money ;
My *fourth* in sugar, but not in honey.
My *fifth* in you, but not in me ;
My *sixth* in little, but not in wee.
My *seventh* in man, but not in boy ;
My *eighth* is less in fast than cloy.
My *whole* is the name of a famous historian.

91. Problem.

A man having a flock of sheep, sold five-sixths of their number; he then bought six more than the number he had left ; then again he sold the one-tenth of the flock he now had, and bought again four more sheep than the one-third of the number he had left just previous to this last purchase. After all this twice selling and buying he had one sheep more than the one-half of the number he had at first. How many had he then ?

92. Rebus.

93. Numerical Enigma.

I am composed of 23 letters:
My 8, 11, 9, 13, 23, 4, 6, 12, 18 is a powerful ruler.
My 10, 19, 1, 7, 2, 21 were ancient priests.
My 5, 22, 20, 8 is a flat, round piece of stone.
My 19, 15 is a pronoun.
My 14, 17, is a great qualifier.
My 16, 14, 11 is a good mollifier.
My *whole* was a distinguished visitor.

94. Homonyms.

a. A convival meeting, a baton, and a card.
b. A mark or target, a boy's nickname, au ornament for a ship, and a useful kitchen utensil.
c. An animal, to carry, to endure, and a constellation.

95. Verbal Puzzle.

Whole, I am an animal; behead and curtail me, and leave repose. Behead me, and leave something used by artists; transpose, and you have to let; curtail, and transpose into a sea animal; transpose again into an auction; behead, and leave a drink.

96. Conundrum.

Why is this like Niagara ?

97. Scriptural Enigma—76 Letters.

20, 66, 59, 66, 82, 48, 70, 65, 67 is a Hebrew word used in one of the first
  twelve chapters of St. Mark.
43, 36, 9, 40, the last word of one of the Proverbs.
9, 23, 15, a type of Christ's kingdom.
29, 71, 19, 74, 55, a sacred number.
27, 57, 24, 72, 54, one of the insignificant men of the Bible.
When was 27, 30, 47, 21 found in a 61, 33, 43, 28 ?
38, 57, 40, 72, 25, one of the canonical books.
34, 37, 75, 13, 22, 9, waters are sweet.
43, 16, 73, 3, 36, 34 is one of the few names mentioned in Revelation.
23, 66, 28, 60, 43, 26, 43 is one of the seven churches of Asia.
41, 1, 68, 66, a musical instrument.
66, 62, 2, 39, a tree.
44, 45, 58, 73, 53, 49,   40, 64, 11, 54, 73, 42, 69, 52, up, 40, 35, 19,
  4, 76, 23, 43 is an incomplete proverb.
7, 30, 34, 53, 40, a famous prophet.
10, 33, 46, 13, a word in the third sentence of the Lord's Prayer.
14, 50, 6, 24, fore-father of Tubal-Cain.
56, 20, 17, 12, to communicate.
Abraham was 5, 8, 4, 51, 71, 63, 26, 18.
31, 36, 61, 37, 44, a word in the verse selected.
  My *whole* is a verse in Leviticus.

98. Names Enigmatically Expressed.

a. Having power. *c.* A kind of oil. *e.* A sign. *g.* A flower.
b. A star. *d.* Favor. *f.* A city. *h.* A bird.

99. Color Puzzle.

Fill the blanks with different colors.

I went over to Mrs. ——ing's store to buy some ——ing to clean my spoons with, and some ——ing for the clothes, and on my way home I called on Mrs. ——ing to ask what kind of ——ing she used, and she gave me some nice ——ing apples.

100. Diagram Puzzle.

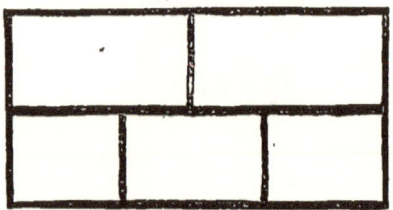

The puzzle is to draw this diagram with *three* strokes of the pencil, without erasing any lines, and without going over the same lines twice.

101. Enigma.

Three very powerful, as well as wonderful instruments.

Instrument No. 1 contains three letters:
> The *first* is found in incompressibility.
> The *second* is found in incombustibility.
> The *third* is found in impenetrability.

Instrument No. 2 is composed of three letters:
> The *first* is found in immalleability.
> The *second* is found in indivisibility.
> The *third* is found in indefensibility.

Instrument No. 3 contains five letters:
> The *first* is found in irresistibility. -
> The *second* is found in incomprehensibility.
> The *third* is found in irrefragibility.
> The *fourth* is found in incorruptibility.
> The *fifth* is found in indestructibility.

The *first* instrument is that inanimate object which, according to the Biblical definition of God, is more like God than any visible inanimate object of which we know.

These three instruments differ very widely in construction, yet, comparatively speaking, the *second* would be almost, if not entirely, useless without the *first;* and the *third* would suffer greatly if the *first* and *second* were wanting. Take away the *third,* and of what lasting service would the *first* and *second* prove?

102. Union Enigma.

1, 8, the abreviation for one of the United States.
3, 5,   "   "   "   "
7, 6,   "   "   "   "
5, 2,   "   "   "   "
2, 4, and k,   "   "   "   "
The *whole* is one of the United States.

103. Double Anagram.

I train all oily cats.
Oh! I nail all city rats.
Each of these lines gives the same word, which shows how the *training* and *nailing* is accomplished.

104. Hidden Implements.

Lord Ragney is dead. A mandrake is sweet. The old shoe is worthless. On the islands of Orkney. Dump low the cart.

105. Numerical Enigma.

I am composed of 25 letters :
My 6, 16, 14, 22 is a period of time.
My 19, 20, 21 is an affirmative.
My 2, 3, 4 is a powerful instrument.
My 9, 8, 7, 24 is an ornament.
My 11, 1, 5 is a boy's nickname.
My 15, 12, 18, 10 is the name of a tree.
My 13, 12, 17, 23, 24, 22 is what every thief is.
My 15, 21, 25 is a cushion.
My *whole* is a proverb.

106. Cross Word.

My *first* is in love, but not in hate ;
My *next* is in fortune, but not in fate.
My *third* is in knife, but not in fork ;
My *fourth* is in eagle, but not in hawk.
My *fifth* is in fun, but not in play ;
My *sixth* is in June, but not in May.
My *seventh* is in letter, but not in note ;
My *eighth* is in vessel, but not in boat.
My *ninth* is in song, but not in ditty ;
My *tenth* is in town, but not in city.
My *whole* is the name of a famous poet ;
I feel quite certain that you know it.

107. Puzzle.

My *whole* is an atrocious crime
　　Condemned by God and human laws ;
Invert it—in two words you find
　　The baleful and the fruitful cause.

108. Rebus.

109. Cross Puzzle.

a. This is an animal sharp.
b. Among weavers ; yarn for the warp.
c. A mineral this will name.
d. To an aeriform fluid next I came.
e. One who goes before ; you will attest.
f. Something without meaning ; the word is used in jest.
g. Authorized this means.
h. A fish found in streams.
i To recede ; becomes my text.
i. A portion of your frame comes next.
k. To decline ; this may be.
　　These form a cross ; the centrals afford
　　Letters that form a cabalistic word ;
　　Supposed to have power to relieve
　　Disease and pain, ancients did believe.

110. Anagrams.

a. How strange!

b. Rent not.

c. Arch gate.

d. Oh! may I act?

e. Up last.

f. Long stave.

g. Enter chasm.

h. Urge boat on.

i. I sail in a pond.

j. Yet left an evil.

k. The scorer.

l. No seat.

m. Taller view.

n. A note.

o. Tear cloth.

p. No city cars.

111. Rebus.

112. Miscellaneous Enigma.

I am composed of 30 letters :

My 33, 27, 13, 23 is a Territory of the United States.

My 11, 7, 30, 26 is a city of great repute.

My 16, 37, 12, 27, 29, 11 is a favorite article of food.

My 9, 19. 34, 7. 11 is what we all should have.

My 22, 6, 21, 21, 16, 11 is a coin.

My 35, 11, 2, 15 is a town in Iowa.

My 34, 10. 18, 24, 30, 12, 8, 29, 11, 31, 13, 30 is the ancient name of a popular city of the United States.

My 25, 13, 14, 28 4, 24 is an idol god of the Hindoos.

My 14, 24, 39, 21 was a king of Israel.

My 12, 38, 31, 32, 30 is a city of ancient times.

My 30, 20, 21, 10 is a beast of burden.

My 5, 17, 11, 27, 21, 10 is an aqueous animal.

My 3, 8, 36, 15 is a post town in Georgia.

My *whole* is a valuable maxim.

113. Arithmetical Puzzle.

From 20 subtract 55, leaving a remainder of 55.

114. Cross Word Enigma.

My *first* is in sheep, but not in lamb ;
My *second* is in goat, but not in ram.
My *third* is in rat, but not in mouse ;
My *fourth* is in stable, but not in house.
My *fifth* is in sea, but not in river ;
My *sixth* is in bow, but not in quiver.
My *seventh* is in bucket, but not in well ;
My *eighth* is in clapper, but not in bell.
My *ninth* is in glade but not in dell.
My *whole* is a town in Virginia.

115. Compound Square Word.

a. A vehicle ; reversed, an inclosure.
b. A girl's name ; reversed, a boy's name.
c. A boy's name ; reversed, a girl's name.
d. A measure ; reversed, used in drawing.

116. Pi.

Hemaun leepop ear ginkees ot former lijas, usesoh fo tirecnocor, oh-samsules dan asnine slumasy. Tub on morfer si lavit hhiwc sode ont hint het knars fo het sascles chiwh lifl hotes ads cluscnosis.

117. Rebus.

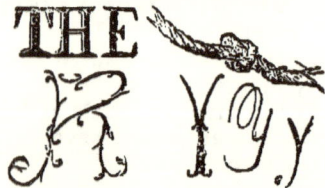

118. Rhyming Answers.

See me now on the throne !
　　Perchance on his brow ;
How famous his name ;
　　He is living there now.
How faded the leaflets !
　　And see where they fall ;
Alas ! in the water,
　　The name of them all.

119. Numerical Enigma.

I am composed of 14 letters :
My 12, 9, 8, 14 is a kind of tree.
My 12, 9, 7, 8 is a measure.
My 1, 2, 6, 5 is an article of clothing.
My 10, 2, 4, 14 is part of the face.
My 4, 5, 11, 2, 13 is an article of furniture.
My *whole* is a European city.

120. Cross Puzzle.

A peer of Scotland.   A time of day.
Equality.   True.
An important organ.   The same as the first.
A consonant.

The peer's name can be read in twelve different ways.

121. Literary Enigma—119 Letters.

The *whole* is a quotation from the distinguished poet, 61, 95, 88, 68, 108, 7, 116, 12, 111, 42, 4, in his beautiful poem, 40, 58, 26, 24, 78, 90, in which, playing a prominent part will be found the character 41, 93, 75, 103, 53, 8.

2, 44, 79, 56, 72, 27, 70, 113, 102, 85, 94, 76, 118, a short poem by Moore.

3, 48, 34, 12, 18, 40, 66, a learned lawyer of England, now deceased.

82, 5, 73, 67, 14, 85, a famous painter who died from excess of laughter.

107 is found in both Homer and Shakespeare, but not in Virgil nor Milton.

74, 77, 21, 13, 89, 37, 1, 33, 10, 25, an eminent American writer and contributor to the *Christian Union*.

23, 47, 32, the initials of an American poet.

54, 62, 80, 43, 9, 112, 6, 92, 117, 63, 55, 83, 10, 28, 119, a poem from the pen of England's present laureate.

109, 114, 50, 59, 30, wrote a history of the United States.

17, 52, 110, 74, 71, 88, an American poet.

99, 105, 97, 51, 50, 81, 106, 98, 100, 19, 51, 87, 104, a poem by Keats.

16, 29, 11, 106, 63, was an eminent Italian poet, and the author of 20, 86, 96, 39, 65, 91, 22, 9, 86, 60, 45, 115, 6, and 81, 15, 19, 57, 46, 64, 84, 101, was the city of his birth.

122. Geographical Puzzle.

By taking one-tenth of Burlington, two-twelfths of Philadelphia, one-eighth of Portugal, one-ninth of Chicago, one-fourth of Rome, one-tenth of Louisville, and two-ninths of Rochester, you will obtain a well-known American city.

123. Illustrated Proverb.

124. Word Puzzle.

I am the name of an honorable occupation, and contain seven letters.
I also contain a general name for seeds, a surly visage, a conjunction, an
instrument to blow with, a border, a kind of liquor, a verb, an edge,
general name of the human race, a foolish smile, name of the ocean, a
circular thing, the atmosphere, a great distance, a fish's membrane, and
profit.

125. Drop-Letter Puzzle.

Every vowel omitted:

.. Rth ..tgr.ws th. myth.c f.nc..s
S.ng b.s.d. h.r .n h.r y..th,
.nd th.s d.b.n..r. r.m.nc.s
S..nd b.t d.ll b.s.d th. tr.th.

126. Cross Word Enigma.

My *first* is in girl, but not in boy ;
My *second* is in boat, but not in toy.
My *third* is in left, but not in right ;
My *fourth* is in falter, but not in flight.
My *fifth* is in six, but not in seven ;
My *sixth* is in twenty, but not eleven ;
My *whole* you may guess if you try,
For it is frequently seen in the sky.

127. Anagram.

Ni hte Aaaicdn dnal, no het sshoer fo eth nsaib fo Snami,
Sdttian, eesciddu, llsit, hte llttie llvgeai fo Gnar-per
Yla ni hte ffrtuilu vylale. Stao swodmea tstrheced ot teh drtsweaa.
Ggiiuo eth alloige sti maen, dna suretap ot flskoc ttwhiou bremun.

128. Geographical Puzzle.

I arose, took a city of England, and, being a country of Europe, desired a city of France to set the mountain in Washington Territory. She placed upon it a river in Missouri, which contained a piece of a river in Iowa seasoned with another river in Missouri, a river in Idaho, and a river in Colorado, for sauce, with a river in Montana to drink. On going to the window I saw that a range of mountains in Africa had disappeared, and the sky, as far as I could see, was a cape on the coast of Ireland, and thought it best to a cape on the coast of England. My maid said that the sky was a sea south of Russia in the channel south of Scotland, and she had a cape off North Carolina, that the day would be a lake north of the United States. I then told her to bring my city in Scotland and I would a cape off North Carolina. She said it was in a bay on the coast of England. This put me in great a cape on the coast of Scotland, and I expostulated with her, when the saucy maid told me to hold my river in Montana, and that a cape on the coast of Maine had the misfortune to get it covered with a country of Asia. I finally took my city of Germany wrap and mount of Oregon, and went out, but soon saw I was doomed to a cape on the coast of Washington Territory, as there were sure indications of a cape on the coast of Oregon. I then took a city in Kansas with the cape of Maine, and decided it was best to give up our journey for that day.

129. Rebus.

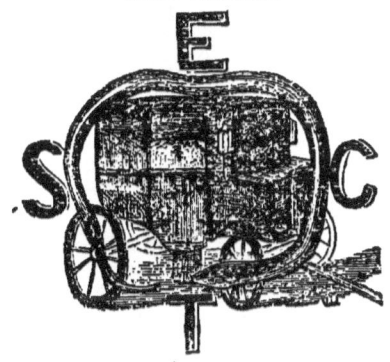

130. Word Changes.

I am a preposition of two letters. Prefix one letter, and I am a near relative; change my head, and I am a Latin prefix; change again, and I mean to put on.

131. Puzzle.

I am 14 letters. I am a bird, a crowned head, a fish, and a sportsman. My *first* resembles me very closely—in fact, it is identical with myself. My *first two* are in the sentence before this. My *first three* would lisp if I could add 49 inches to them. My *first four* is a game that the boys delight in. My *fourth, fifth,* and *sixth* is the name of somebody's mother, wife, sister, and daughter. My *three last* suggest the Celestial empire. My *last eight* embrace a vehicle, an insect, and a favorite decoction; also a plant. I am between my *seventh* and *eighth,* and while I am there, there is but one meaning to us three, no matter if you spell us backwards or forwards.

132. Rebus.

133. Cross Word.

My *first* is in short, but not in tall ;
My *next* is in sport, but not in ball.
My *third* is in money, but not in gold ;
My *fourth* is in modest, but not in bold.
My *fifth* is in joy, but not in fun ;
My *sixth* is in muffins, but not in bun.
My *seventh* is in blue, but not in brown ;
My *eighth* is in city, but not in town.
My *ninth* is in knuckle, but not in hand ;
My *tenth* is in clay, but not in sand.
My *eleventh* is in minute, but not in hour ;
With my *whole* the poet has twined the bower.

134. Geographical Puzzle.

Behead the first syllable of a river in a Southern State, and leave an animal; behead the second, and leave part of the body. Curtail the first, and leave a covering ; transpose the second, and leave food.

135. Charade.

The preacher's boast, the Gentile's friend,
 The Christian and the martyr :
The saint who could his comfort vend,
 But ne'er his honor barter.
This is my *first*, and 'mong the first
 Of Christian saints you'll find him ;
A name to them once so accursed,
 Of glory now reminds them.
My *second* you have used full oft
 When at your meals reclining ;
A seasoning to some dainty viand
 When breakfasting or dining.
My *third* the cattle crop each day,
 As through the meadow going ;
Their tinkling bell keeps joyous tune
 With pent-up herds' deep lowing.
My *whole's* a famous *nom de plume*
 Of one of Ireland's authors,
Who pictured well the virtue of
 Her suffering sons and daughters.

136. Miscellaneous Enigma.

I am composed of 27 letters :
My 13, 26, 7, 9 is a way.
My 14, 26, 8, 10, 12, 27 is a mythological character.
My 19, 11, 2, 13, 5 means unearthly.
My 6, 2, 25, 24, 23 means clever, satirical.
My 16, 17, 8, 27, 1 was a celebrated Scotch poet.
My 4, 7, 21 is a portion of the human body.
My 18, 15, 14, 20, 27, 5 is a traditionary tale.
My 9, 2, 7, 27, 7 was a goddess of mythology.
My 13, 12, 17, 10, 11 is a cosmetic.
My *whole* is the name of a celebrated author, recently dead.

137. Biblical Anagrams.

a. Only a biban, a kind of brick.
b. Se calm, a kind of furniture.
c. I map yrds., found in America and Egypt.
d. Baar, a kind of oven.
e. We dash erb, a kind of bread.
f. Do to le si lo he rn ths, an inscription in six ancient alphabets.

138. Entomological.

The cook's insect; the dairy insect; the widow's insect; the spirit insect; the tree insect; the runaway insect; the flaming insect; the insect to pound with; uncle's insect; the grammatical insect; the ball-player's insect; herbage, and part of a mill; a winged serpent insect; extinction of life, and a time-peace; a Bible mountain, and a snare; a girl's name, and a verb.

139. Rebus.

140. Historical Enigma.

I am composed of 89 letters:

My 26, 29, 30, 5, 89 was the name of a French painter of great distinction.

My 9, 3, 7, 12, 22, 2, 32, 35, 8 was the name of a governor of the British possessions in India, he was impeached for maladministration.

My 89, 14, 8, 19, 10, 33, 3 was the name of a celebrated French authoress.

My 6, 4, 15, 7, 24 is the name of a fortress in the United States, famous in the history of Texan independence.

My 23, 16, 21, 35, 11, 4, 2, 88 was the name of a celebrated American philosopher and statesman.

My 1, 2, 36, 18, 24, 28 was the name of a professor in the University of Edinburgh, Scotland, but is better known as the principal editor of "Blackwood's Magazine," and its chief contributor.

My 13, 8, 37, 19, 81 was the name of an illustrious Grecian philosopher.

My 85, 2, 24, 5, 28 was the name of a celebrated mathematician of Naples.

My 23, 17, 25, 89, 5, 28, 10, 32, 26 was the name of a King of Spain.

My 85, 17, 12, 8, 14, 20 was the name of a wicked governor of Switzerland, who was killed by the celebrated William Tell.

My 6, 35, 20, 24, 32 was the name of the most noted of the Illyrian Pirates.

My *whole* is the name and birth-place of a celebrated poet.

141. Decapitations.

a Behead a town in New York and leave a boy's name.

b. Behead a country of Europe and leave anguish.

c. Behead a river in Italy and leave a vowel.

d. Behead a country of Europe and leave another.

e. Behead a division of Germany and leave a town in Arabia.

f. Behead a river of France, and leave a stone used for sharpening instruments.

142. Literary Enigma—159 Letters.

84, 103, 151, 22, 94. 83, 108, 103, 13, 30, 55 is a pleasing English poetess.

143, 48, 46, 126, 149, 93, 84, 118, 80, 52, 106, 80, 99 is the author of "Ginx's Baby."

152, 144, 85, 106, 28, 2, 155, 13, 38, 139, 64, 81 is one of the brightest of our American lady writers.

34, 62, 132, 62, 96, 158, 19, 5, 71, 88 is one of Disraeli's works.

136, 46, 11, 53, 111, 26, 77, 89, 105, 141, 59, 114 is the *nom de plume* of the author of "Lucille."

159, 131, 121, 134, 108, 76, 69, 130. 68, 138, 153, 91, 80 was a dramatist of the seventeenth century and the earliest translator of Homer.

40, 57, 23, 67, 17, 12, 157, 54, 9, 106, 87, 101, 24, 75, 121, 117 is one of Dickens' works.

124, 47, 78, 86, 21 is a character in "Romola."

42. 82, 123, 133 is a humorous American poet.

140, 187, 39, 20, 58, 97, 98, 16, 6, 50 is a German novelist.

74, 125, 49, 44, 93, 147 is an English historian.

109, 146. 27, 116, 137, 152, 150 is one of the cleverest of American essayists.

145, 104, 36, 84, 85, 73, 156 is a popular young English novelist.

7, 112, 135 is a young American poet, author and lecturer.

43, 41, 148, 1, 24 was a Scotch poet.

43, 65, 61, 3, 60, 8, 102, 31, 110 is a new American poet and author.

127, 148, 4, 66, 52, 72, 10, 14, 15, 52 is a noted artist and caricaturist.

38, 25, 18, 32. 69, 122, 77 was an old English poet.

45, 37, 111, 40, 28, 10, 56, 29. 51, 154, 65 is a poem by Burns.

150, 23, 111, 4, 50, 23, 79, 115, 81, 6, 9 is an English dramatist.

13, 70, 90. 100, 57, 11, 23, 40, 5, 12, 27, 120 is a character in one of Dickens' works.

57, 113, 128, 129, 40, 63 is an English novelist, recently deceased.

153, 30, 28, 89, 5, 92, 116, 2, 27, 95, 142, 89, 5, 9 is one of Ruskin's works.

84 6. 107, 119, 113, 46, 86, 76, 80 is a character in "Our Mutual Friend"

103, 83, 60, 115, 13, 39, 43 41, 77 was a famous sword mentioned by Tennyson in "Idyls of the King."

My *whole* is one of the sayings of George Eliot in "Adam Bede."

143. Scriptural Puzzle.

Make the following letters a verse in Proverbs:

```
A  S  A  N  N  E
O  T  S  R  T  H
F  WU  H  T  B
E  T  A  A  U  W
R  W  R  T  S  O
A  W  G  U  R  U
Y  R  O  D  R  P
I  V  S  I  A  E
E  S  T  N  G  R
```

144. An Aviary.

What bird is formed by a market and a preposition ?   Omit one letter in the name of an aquatic fowl and leave a number.   Take the alternate letters of a bird found in the Arctic regions, and you have an exclamation and a preposition.   The alternate letters of a sea-fowl form what insect ?   Behead and curtail a bird, and you have an entreaty ; or omit the centre letter, read backward, and you have an adjective signifying close.

145. Enigma, Whittier's Poems—93 Letters.

66, 34, 76, 38, 73, 55, 38, 50, 69, 47 is a graceful twining plant celebrated by Whittier.

55, 6, 38 90, 56, 77, 55, 62, 33, 48, a friend of Whittier,-who went South.

55, 37, 46. 18, 84, 29, 21, 75, 64, 86, one of the sweetest girls in Whittier's family.

93, 65, 81, 28, 59, 78, 60, 36, 31 would be unpleasant for one living in a 61, 39, 17, 2, 7, 53, 5. 34, 92, 59, 35, 62, 49, 3.

41, 45, 74. 74, 64, 91, 22, 71, a river.

59, 29, 21, 89, 79, 19, 10. 26, 59, 86, 23, and 55, 62, 82, 13, 55, 20, 90, 12, 58, 68 are two of Whittier's brain-children who neglected the 25, 8, 27, 92, 55, 52, 57, 67, 80, 40.

64, 53. 88, 9, 34, 85, 44, 90, 54, 52, 80, 51 did not prove Whittier's 55, 43, 18, 83, 64, 8, 55, 88, 34.

26, 86, 49, 82 is a dedication.

31, 70, 15, 59, 12, 24, 3, 22, 37, 54, 92, 87, 72, 63, 4, 57. 22, 1, 42, 17, 89, 28, 59, 11, 16, 80, an active little animal with rather too much brain.

59, 89, 65, 39, 87, 64, 49, 64, 5, 35 is suggested at the mention of Whittier's name.

The *whole* is a sentence from Shakespeare respectfully commended to the politicians of the present day.

146. Hidden Counties and Cities.

Poverty revels in winter.
Do not go into the bear's den, Mark.
What kind of timber ? Linden, of course.
The sun is warm in hay-time.
Lida, bold Selim while I drink.
When I have looked at the picture of the Virgin I am going home.

147. Concealed Rivers.

a. He owns two horses, one is a dun and the other a bay.
b. Praise I need, scolding discourages me.
c. Our honey is considered the best in the village.
d. At one time he made snares for sale.
e. Did you see what fine fruit he brought me.
f. It is very pleasant here in dusty weather.
g. It is the same in Amanda's house.
h. I never saw a pale native.

148. Charade.

In my *first* my fare I reckoned;
 At my *second* stopped to dine;
Then approached my *first* and *second,*
 Where I bought my *third* of twine;
With it I wandered over hill and knoll,
Collecting species to fill my *whole.*

149. Numerical Enigma.

I am composed of 20 letters:
My 6, 4, 11, 8, 3 is to hesitate.
My 5, 10, 13, 9 is a member of the body.
My 12, 20, 1, 2, 9 is a fish.
My 14, 7, 19, 15 is what we must do if we would live.
My 17, 16, 18 is a horse.
My *whole* is a wholesome proverb.

150. Anagrams on Authors' Names.

a. Sam, I will speak, hear.   *b.* Silver hog, mould it.

151. Puzzles.

a. N. E. Ces cit yis them O. T.   Hero fin V. E. Nt Ion.

b. Fifty-one votes please bring,
 And change them to flowers of spring.

152. Pi.

Nobuttririe hoguth tale moces ta slat

153. Problem.

A circular fishpond takes up just one acre of ground. What length of halter, fastened to the edge of the water, will allow a horse just liberty to graze an acre of grass ?

154. Birds in the Clouds.

In a saucepan, serve up the soup.
My pet, rely upon me.
The Turk eyed him closely.
Jane must learn.
How happy every little child.
Man, unless good, is miserable.
Ann, I asked you.
Pa, vote for me.
I left my muff in Charleston.
John is a good man, a kind husband.

Fagan and Uria Heep.
Sam is an odd young man.
To go to Tamaqua, Illinois.
Sambo was a brave negro.
My hens nip every bud.
Did you ever see a wasp in Kansas ?
Keep your dust in town.
The cows wandered far away.
Kate, Alfred, and Sue.

155. Word Squares.

I.

A sovereign.
A thought.
A structure which only a certain class
    of animals can make.
A kind of door.

II.

Tardy.
The contents of a surface.
A secretion.
A nobleman.

156. Arithmetical Problem.

A farmer, taking 100 bushels potatoes to market, sold the first 6 bushels thereof at 80 cents per bushel ; after which sale he made four more sales, one after the other, increasing each time the number of bushels sold the previous sale in geometrical proportion ratio, whereof said first 6 bushels sold was the first term. But every subsequent sale he dropped 5 cents per bushel in the price. Thus, having sold the first 6 bushels at 80 cents per bushel, he sold the next lot at 75 cents per bushel, the third lot at 70 cents per bushel, the fourth lot at 65 cents per bushel, and the fifth lot at 60 cents per bushel. After which he sold the remainder of what he had left of said 100 bushels at 50 cents per bushel, and after laying out in town, for various merchandise bought, $2.82½ cents of this his potato money, he yet brought home $60 in cash. Can any mathematician tell me the number of bushels he had sold at the last sale at 50 cents per bushel ?

157. Scriptural Acrostic.

The initials form a pass-word:
One who dwelt in the top of a rock.
Whose carpenters built a house for David?
Who became a servant.under tribute?
Where God talked with a' man.
Who was sent to Antioch?
The name of a rock.
The name of a well.
A place of vineyards.
A city that was forgotten for seventy years.
A land containing gold and surrounded by a river.

158. Historical Enigma—57 Letters.

10, 44, 14, 3, 52, 54, an English consort.
7, 39, 55, 49, 15, 1, 2, 45, 42, 9, 57, a French king.
18, 5, 35, 6, an English queen.
30, 22, 24, 11, 18, a Roman emperor.
41, 20, 18, 28, 29, 17, a beautiful ancient queen.
23, 31, 56, 26, an English title.
27, 22, 52, 1, 55, 8, 35, a king of Rome.
12, 14, 36, 17, 44, 57, 46, the name of two kings of the seventeenth century.
56, 36, 48, 16, 19, 43, 47, a famous English nobleman.
53, 32, 40, 17, 34, 33, an English king.
46, 51, 8, 5, 25, a river on which a renowned city is situated.
4, 5, 37, 12, 35, where Moreau defeated the Austrians.
50, 38, 10 was brought to Europe by the Dutch, in 1610.
The *whole* is an historical fact.

159. Diagonals.

To gather slowly.
Something preserved in remembrance.
A cave and a verb.
A valued friend of Napoleon I.
Leaves of a plant, used as a medicine.

160. Puzzle.

My *first*, and *second, third, fourth*, and *fifth*
    May all be found in "search;"
Then add to these my *first* and *second*,
    And my *last* is seen in "lurch;"
My *whole* is a name you've often read
    Of a great astronomer long since dead.

161. Cross Word.

My *first* is in mud, but not in dirt;
My *second* is in cape, but not in skirt.
My *third* is in time, but not in clock;
My *fourth* is in hood, but not in frock.
My *fifth* in Henry, but not in Harry;
My *sixth* in Emma, but not in Carrie.
My *seventh* in panther, but not in roe;
My *eighth* in tiger, but not in doe.
My *ninth* in hinges, but not in door.
My *tenth* in calix, but not in flower;
My *eleventh* in steeple, but not in tower.
　Study me that you may know my relations.

162. Geographical Combination.

a. To tear asunder, and that which we walk upon.
b. Two consonants between two pronouns.
c An American, a fruit, and a verb.
d. Part of a year, and one-third of a month.
e. A man's name, and a weight.
f. An animal, and a craft.
g. A fruit, and a preposition.
h. A loud noise, and a propeller.
i. Part of a rat, a relative, and a preposition.
j. A plant, and a beverage between two consonants.

163. Transposed Proverb.

Go see honey market, ma'am.

164. Charade.

A sportsman started out one day,
　With fishing-rod, and line, and hook;
He to my *second* made his way,
　And threw his line into the brook.

He sat himself beneath my *whole;*
　Before him ran the murmuring stream;
A languor soft stole o'er his soul,
　And he began to think and dream.

When suddenly he felt his line—
　An exclamation from him burst;
He quickly responded to the sign,
　And safely landed there my *first.*

165. Decapitations.

a. Behead a cape in North Carolina and leave an adjective, signifying empty, hollow.

b. Behead a cape on the cost of Florida and leave an adjective, signifying to have the power.

c Behead a river in Louisiana and leave a boy's nickname.

d. Behead a river in Turkey and leave a girl's name.

e. Behead a city in France and leave composure.

f. Behead a city in Delaware and leave across.

g. Behead a river in Mississippi and leave a nobleman's title.

h. Behead a river in Idaho and leave a bird.

i. Behead an island on the coast of Asia and leave a domestic animal.

j. Behead a cape in British America and leave a kind of playing card.

166. Puzzle.

I am composed of five parts, head, body, two legs and tail. Cut off my head, and you have a well-known element; cut off my head and body, and you have a verb expressing a very common action; cut off my head, body, and left leg, and you have a simple preposition; cut off my head, right leg and tail, and you have a personal pronoun of the masculine gender; cut off my body, right leg, and tail, and you have a personal pronoun of the first person, plural number; cut off my left leg, and you have a word which may be used in eight different ways; cut off my body and right leg, and you have an adjective expressing a soaked state; cut off my head and left leg, and you have a very useful article. Turn me over and cut off head and body, and you have the name of a beverage.

The *whole* is the name of a grain.

167. Proverb Hash.

Out of the following thirty-one words make five well known proverbs:

A new debt is no stone.   Out of that never a horse glitters.
Look not out of the mouth.   All rolling gold sweeps moss clean.
A gift broom gathers in danger.

168. Positives and Comparatives.

a. A quadruped, to shrink.   *e.* Faction, a beverage.
b. Formal, a small book.   *f.* Part of a garment, a pickle.
c. A sea fish, to remain long.   *g.* To gather, hue.
d Import, a vessel.

ANSWERS.

1. The celebration of the centennial of the Declaration of American Independence.

2. *a.* Obstroperous.   *b.* Rotundas.   *c.* Unnoticed.   *d.* Penetential.   *e.* Counterparts.   *f.* Insignificant.   *g.* Enslaver.   *h.* Sentimental.   *i.* Apostrophes.   *j.* Gratification.

3. Sunday-school.

4. Hood, Opie, Oils, Desk.

5. Venison.

6. Mouse, Ouse, Use, Se (See), E.

7. Wasps, Asp, Raven, Ave, Lion, Io, Bears, Ears, Wren (Sir Christopher), Scallop, Mice, Ice.

8.
A	B	E	L
B	E	L	A
E	L	A	M
L	A	M	B

9. To thy own self be true.

10. Marsh.

11. Thou shalt not take the name of the Lord thy God in vain.

12. 95.680536 rods.   80.567934 "   23.75153 "   and   87.6528 rods.   93.622461 "   18.724739 "

13. Never faint or falter.

14. Spain.

15. All the labor of man is for his mouth, and yet the appetite is not filled.

16. "Lives of great men all remind us
    We may make our lives sublime,
    And departing, leave behind us
    Footsteps on the sands of time."

17. *a.* Rose.   *b.* Lily.   *c.* Violet.   *d.* Daisy.   *e.* Opal.   *f.* Garnet.   *g.* Diamond.   *h.* Pearl.

18. *a.* Shoeblack.   *b.* Applejack.

19. The Future.

20. *a.* Veterinarian.   *b.* Fermentative.   *c.* Impenetrable.   *d.* Surprised.   *e.* Wearisome.   *f.* Restraining.   *g.* Antagonism.   *h.* Misinterpret.   *i.* Nonsensical.   *j.* Indemnified.

21. Lake Pontchartrain.

22. Horace Greeley.

23. 109)79842(32 (Key—Forest Lawn).

24 A word fitly spoken is like apples of gold in pictures of silver.

25. "We look before and after,
    And pine for what is not;
    Our sincerest laughter
    With some pain is fraught;
Our sweetest songs are those that tell of saddest thought."

26. Penknife.
27. Civil.
28. Because he is snowed in (is no din.)
29. *a.* Huntsville. *b.* Belmont. *c.* Little Rock. *d.* Traverse. *e.* Los Angelos. *f.* Salt Lake. *g.* Litchfield. *h.* Roseburg. *i.* Montgomery. *j.* Prescott. *k.* Marysville. *l.* Marquett.
30. Colorado.
31. 156, 240, and 252 perches.
32. Sawdust pills cure many diseases.
33. Zone, Tone, Lone, Hone, Gone, Cone.

34.

```
S    arsaparill   A
I    nūde         L
R    oo           F
W    a'           R
A    l            E
L    ea           D
T    ournamen     T
E    squir        E
R    ai           N
S    u            N
C    anop         Y
O    ptic         S
T    obacc        O
T    alo          N
```

35. Wheat, Heat, Eat.
36. Presence of mind is at all times necessary.
37. Estate, State, Ate, Tea, East, Taste, Sea, Sate.
38. Anne, Verse, Sairy (Sairy Gamp)—Anniversary.
39. *a.* The Window. *b.* Because they have ears which cannot hear, and eyes which cannot see. *c.* Because it is one of the greatest composers of modern times. *d.* When it is a little palo (pail). *e.* Because, if he got a wife, his principles would not allow him to sup-porter.
40. Miss Ouri and Miss Issippi.

41.

I.					II.				III.		
A	M	P	L	E	B	E	A	M	B	I	R	D
M	E	L	O	N	E	A	S	E	I	D	E	A
P	L	A	N	T	A	S	I	A	R	E	A	M
L	O	N	G	E	M	E	A	N	D	A	M	E
E	N	T	E	R

42. Can a woman forget her sucking child?

43.	
Ishmael.	Og.
Nimrod.	Uzza.
Cyrus.	Rimmon.
Rephaiah.	Felix.
Eli.	Asahel.
Ahab.	Ishbi-benob.
Shamgar.	Tou
Ezra.	Hezekiah.

44. *a.* Oxford *b.* Galena. *c.* Naples. *d.* Dover *e.* Tyre. *f.* Ava. *g.* Thebes *h.* Troy.

45. Honor thy father and thy mother, that thy days may be long upon the land which the Lord thy God giveth thee.

46. No(o;se, Cl(e)an, Dr(e)am, F(r)ame.

47. 99 9-9.

48. " Let us then be what we are, and speak what we think, and in all things keep ourselves loyal to truth and the sacred professions of friendship "

49. Life is sweet.

50. *a.* Commit. *b.* Concordance. *c.* Crop. *d.* Crow. *e.* Cue. *f.* Cockle. *g.* Dam.

51. The straight road is always the shortest and surest.

52. The letter D.

53. Our reputation depends greatly upon the choice of our companions.

54. Stew, Pie, Dye, Tie (Stupidity).

55. Woodbine.

56. SepaRated, JacObin, unCle, sHe, E, aSp, asTer, revErse, reveRence – Rochester.

57. The proverb respecting "strong drink," is Prov. xxiii. 32. The proverb respecting "prudence of speech," is Prov. xxix. 2. The proverb respecting "good and evil," is Prov. xiii. 21· The proverb respecting "forbearance," is Prov. xv. 1. The *whole* is "He that walketh in his uprightness feareth the Lord, but he that is perverse in his ways despiseth him."

58. Trustees.

59. *a.* William M. Thackeray. *b.* Elizabeth B. Browning. *c.* Horace Greeley. *d.* Oliver Cromwell. *e.* Noah Webster. *f.* Wilkie Collins.

> 60. My *first* is the name of a poet
> Whose motto was always my *second ;*
> My *whole* the finest of language is reckoned —Poe-try.

61. A cat may look at a king.

62. *a.* Identifying. *b.* Commensurate. *c.* Articulates. *d.* Enterprise. *e.* Coincides. *f.* Gladiator *g.* Repugnant *h.* Universal. *i.* Atheistic. *j.* Stockholder.

63. Sewing, Swing, Sing, Sin, In, I.

64. F(ox)-g(love.)

65. Nightingale (Knight, Night, Night in Gale.)

66. TurbiD, EbullitioN, LavA, EnougH, GluT, RafteR, AllegrO, ParisH, HollandS, Telegraph, Shorthand.

67. A.'s speed, four miles an hour; B.'s three.

68. $801 90.

69. Be not deceived ; evil communications corrupt good manners.– 1 Corinthians, chap. xv., verse 33.

70. Tiglathpileser.

71. I was going on a journey, so I went out to prepare for it. First, I purchased a piece of Astrakan for an outside wrap, and some Cologne for its perfume. I asked the clerk for my bill, and he said the sum was a Guinea. I passed on, and soon met a Peer of Belgium looking for some Nice fowls, which he had seen flying through the Air(e) : but could not see to throw a Stone, because the Air(e) was so full of Smoke. I went into another store, and asked a Man if he had any Pearl-colored silk, of which I bought enough for a dress, and a Hood to top off with. I then went back to my Castle (Cassel), and began packing my provisions. My box was made of Red Cedar, to keep its contents from Worms. I filled it with a piece

of Buffalo, an Egg, some Salt, Spice, Onion, and Bourbon. I told a Lassie (Lassa) to do up some Nankin, and see if the box was full. It was full, and just then I heard Allen at the door, and found that a Negro was holding my horse. I took a Lily (Lille) which was in full bloom, for a friend, and departed, after receiving a Farewell from all my friends.

72. Barefoot men should not tread on thorns.

73. What are thoughts? A wind-swept meadow,
Mimicking a troubled sea;
Are not life and death a shadow
From the rock eternity?

74. *a.* Scamp, Lamp, Gamp, Cramp, Tramp, Damp, Clamp, Camp. *b.* Double, Stubble, Trouble, Bubble. *c.* Table, Babel, Fable, Abel, Gable, Cable, Sable.

75. Cato.

76 An epitaph on a woman who sold earthen-ware.
Beneath this stone lies Katharine Gray,
Changed from a busy life to lifeless clay;
By earth and clay she got her pelf,
And now she's turned to earth herself.
Ye weeping friends, let me advise,
Abate your grief and dry your eyes;
For what avails a flood of tears !
Who knows but in a run of years,
In some tall pitcher or broad pan,
She in her shop may be again ?

77. Martha's Vineyard, in which may be found: 1. Aar. 2. Rtysh. 3. Aras. 4. Trave. 5. Ems. 6. Mayn. 7. Iser. 8 Rhine. 9. Save. 10. Shary. 11. Rca. 12. Thames. 13. Tyne. 14. Ayr 15. Tay. 16. Aras. 17. Red. 18. Tar. 19. Daw. 20. Sivan. 21. Van. 22. Maravi. 23. Rainy. 24. Havre. 25. Syra. 26. Athens. 27. Sana. 28. Aden. 29. Herat. 30. Ava. 31. Athens. 32. Darian.

78. Buckwheat cakes.

79. MacaucO, AlligatoR, CabaI, CockatoO, AngeL, WhalE—Maccaw, Oriole.

80. Wine is a mocker, strong drink is raging.

81. Railroad crossing.

82 Paint, a Pint; Weird, Wider, Wired; Lime, Mile.

83. B E A M
E A S E
A S I A
M E A T

84. *a.* Christopher Columbus *b.* Daniel Boone. *c.* Abraham Lincoln. *d.* Henry Ward Beecher. *e.* Louis Napoleon. *f.* S. F. B. Morse. *g.* U. S. Grant. *h.* Charles Dickens. *i.* Harriet Beecher Stowe.

85. *a.* Kingfisher. *b.* Crow. *c.* Toucan. *d.* Bluejay. *e.* Nightingale. *f.* Plover (clover).

86. Beauty draws more than oxen.

87. Eight o'clock, P. M.

88. Snow, Now, Ow, W; Son, Won, Own.

89. *a.* Brest. *b.* Leon. *c.* Oporto. *d.* Coblentz. *e.* Granada. *f.* Perth. *g.* Cherbourg. *h.* Berne.

90. Macaulay.

91. 52 – (having at first 102).

92. A rose would smell as sweet by any other name.

93. Grand Duke Alexis, of Russia.

94. *a.* Club. *b.* Jack. *c.* Bear.

95. Wensel, Ease, Easel, Lease, Seal, Sale, Ale.

96. It is a cat erect (cataract).

97. "And if a man will redeem at all aught of his tithes, he shall add thereto the fifth part thereof."

98. *a.* Abel. *b* Stella. *c.* Olive. *d.* Grace. *e.* Mark *f.* Florence. *g.* Rose. *h.* Martin.

99. Redding, Whiting, Blueing, Browning, Blacking, Greening.

100. Hold a square piece of paper in the fingers of both hands; fold it over from top to bottom once, making it appear half its former size; fold it again from right to left, so that when shut up like a book the upper edges will exactly meet their entire length. The paper now appears one-quarter of its first size; measure off from the folded corner upon these two folded edges, a distance less than half to their termini, and fold the pages back upon themselves, so that the whole upper edge shall be contiguous as far as they go. If the paper be dropped now upon the table, these contiguous edges will spread and take the form of a letter W. Opening the paper now to its original size, the creases made in the folding will be represented by the dotted lines in the following diagram :

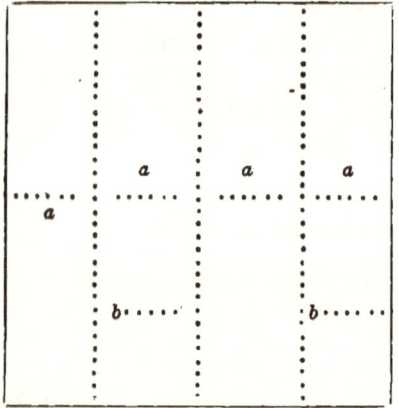

Fold again, as before, and it will be observed that the lines *a, a, a, a,* become contiguous to each other, as also do the lines *b, b,* and that *a, a, a, a,* are still at right angles with *b, b.* Now, pressing these edges closely together, with the left thumb and forefinger, mark with a pencil, and with one stroke, the edges that formed W, and the edges at right angels. This forms a figure like this :

Then, with one stroke of the pencil, make the outer edge, then, with one stroke, make the figure complete.

101. Sun, Eye, Bible.
102. Maryland.
103. *Rat*ionalistically.
104. Drag, Rake, Hoe, Fork, Plow.
105. A penny saved is a penny earned.
106. Longfellow.
107. Murder, Red, Rum.
108. Tenants and trees leave about the 1st of May.

109.
```
          C A T
          A B B
          O R E
          G A S
P R E D E C E S S O R
A B R A C A D A B R A
P R E C E D E N T E D
          G A R
          E B B
          A R M
          S A G
```

110. *a.* Hagerstown.   *b.* Trenton.   *c.* Carthage.   *d.* Omaha City.   *e.* St. Paul.
f. Galveston.   *g.* Manchester.   *h.* Baton Rouge.   *i.* Indianapolis.   *j.* Fayetteville.
k. Rochester.   *l.* Easton.   *m.* Waterville.   *n.* Eaton.   *o.* Charlotte.   *p.* Carson City.

111. Continue in holiness.
112. Do unto others as you would have them do unto you.

113.
$$\frac{X\ X}{5\ 5}$$
5 5

114 Strasbourg.

115.
```
a. D R A Y
b. R O S A
c. A S O R
d. Y A R D
```

116. Humane people are seeking to reform jails, houses of correction, alms houses, and insane asylums. But no reform is vital which does not thin the ranks of the classes which fill those sad seclusions.

117. The over-curious are not over-wise.

118. Crown, Frown, Renown, Town, Brown, Down, Drown, Noun.

119. Constantinople.

```
120. G l e n e l G
       L e v e L
         E y E
           N
         E v E
       L o y a L
     G l e n e l G
```

121. "The tear, down childhood's cheek that flows,
Is like the dew-drop on the rose ;
When next the summer breeze comes by,
And waves the bush, the flower is dry."

122. Baltimore.

123. "He who follows a toad may fall into a ditch."

124. Farming.

125. Earth out-grows the mythic fancies
Sung beside her in her youth,
And those debonaire romances
Sound but dull beside the truth.

126. Galaxy.

127. In the Acadian land, on the shores of the basin of Minas,
Distant, secluded, still, the little village of Grand-pre
Lay in the fruitful valley. Vast meadows stretched to the eastward.
Giving the village its name, and pasture to flocks without number.

128. I arose, took a Bath, and, being Hungary, told Nancy to set the Table. She placed upon it a Platte, a piece of Turkey, seasoned with Salt, some Salmon, Cherry sauce, with Milk to drink. I saw the Snow had disappeared, the sky Clear, and thought it best to Start. My maid said the sky was Black in the North, and she had a Fear that the day would be Rainy. I then told her to bring my Parsley and I would Look-out. She said it was in The Wash. This put me in great Wrath, when the saucy maid told me to hold my Tongue, that Elizabeth had the misfortune to get it covered with Greece. I then took my Berlin wrap and Hood and went out, but soon saw I was doomed to Disappointment, as there were indications of Foul weather. I took Council with Elizabeth, and decided to stay at home.

128. Cochineal insect.

130. On, Son, Con, Don.

131. *Ispida gigantea.*

132. It's never too late to mend.

133. Honeysuckle.

134. Cape Fear.

135. Paul Peppergrass.

136. Sir Edward George Bulwer Lytton.

137. *a.* Babylonian brick. *b.* Camel's furniture   *c.* Pyramids.   *d.* Arab oven. *e.* Shew-bread. *f.* "Holiness to the Lord."

138. Spider. Butterfly. Mite. Spectre. Locust. Flea. Fire-fly. Beetle. Ant. Bee (be). Cricket. Grass-hopper. Dragon-fly. Death-watch. Hor-net. Katy-did.

139. Incapacity.

140. William Shakespeare, Stratford-on-Avon, England.

141. *a.* Troy—Roy. *b.* Spain—Pain. *c.* Po—O. *d.* Prussia—Russia. *e.* Baden--Aden. *f.* Rhone--Hone.

142. "Nature has her language, and she is not unveracious, but we don't know all the intricacies of her syntax just yet, and in a hasty reading we may happen to extract the very opposite of her real meaning."

143. Commence at the first letter of the upper left hand corner and read: "A soft answer turneth away wrath, but grievous words stir up anger."

144. Mart-in. Te(r)n. Loon (lo! on). Gannet. R-ave-n: Near.

145. "The Pumpkin." "My Playmate." "Mary Garvin." "Snowbound" "Tent on the Beach." "Our River." "Barefoot Boy." "Maud Muller." "Shoemakers." "In School Days." "My Triumph." "To C. S." "Double-headed Snake of Newbury." "Benedicite"--"O, that you could turn your eyes towards the napes of you necks, and make but an interior survey of your good selves."

146 Tyre. Denmark. Berlin. Hayti. Idaho. Virginia.

147 *a.* Duna. *b.* Seine. *c.* Rhone. *d.* Desma. *e.* Ebro. *f.* Indus. *g.* Meinam. *h.* Lena.

148. Cabinet.

149. Out of debt, out of danger.

150. *a.* William Shakespeare. *b.* Oliver Goldsmith.

151. *a.* Necessity is the mother of invention. *b.* Violets (LI VOTES transposed).

152. Retribution, though late, comes at last.

153. 8.93438 rods×rods.

154. *a.* Anser. *b.* Petrel. *c.* Turkey. *d.* Emu. *e.* Pye. *f.* Nun. *g.* Nias. *h.* Paro. *i.* Finch. *j.* Manakin. *k.* Nandu. *l.* Noddy. *m.* Quail. *n.* Raven. *o.* Snipe. *p.* Spink. *q.* Stint. *u.* Swan. *r.* Teal.

155.

I.				II.			
K	I	N	G	L	A	T	E
I	D	E	A	A	R	E	A
N	E	S	T	T	E	A	R
G	A	T	E	E	A	R	L

156. 20⅔ Bushels.

157. Shibboleth.

158. Queen Elizabeth's era is called "the Golden Age" of English literature.

159.

G	l	e	a	N
R	E	l	I	c
D	e	N	i	s
D	U	r	O	c
S	e	n	n	A

160. Herschel.

161. Mathematics.

162. *a.* Cleveland. *b.* Memphis. *c.* Indianapolis (Indian-apple-is). *d.* Augusta (May). *e.* Charleston. *f.* Newark (gnu). *g.* Dayton (date). *h.* Bangor. *i.* Taunton. *j.* Hempstead.

163. Money makes the mare go.

164. Bass-wood.

165. *a.* Clear—Lear. *b.* Sable—Able. *c.* Red—Ed. *d.* Pruth—Ruth. *e.* Brest—Rest. *f.* Dover—Over. *g.* Pearl—Earl. *h.* Clark—Lark. *i.* Fox—Ox. *j.* Race—Ace.

166. Wheat.

167. *a.* A new broom sweeps clean. *b.* Never look a gift horse in the mouth. *c.* All is not gold that glitters. *d.* A rolling stone gathers no moss. *e.* Out of debt, out of danger.

168. *a.* Cow—Cower. *b.* Prim-Primer. *c.* Ling—Linger. *d.* Sense—Censer. *e.* Side—Cider. *f.* Cape—Caper. *g.* Cull—Color.

Good Books Mailed on Receipt of Price.

Art of Ventriloquism.—Contains simple and full directions by which any one may acquire this amusing art, with numerous examples for practice. Also instructions for making the magic whistle, for imitating birds, animals, and peculiar sounds of various kinds. Any boy who wishes to obtain an art by which he can develop a wonderful amount of astonishment, mystery, and fun, should learn Ventriloquism, as he easily can by following the simple secret given in this book. Mailed for 15 cents.

Magic Trick Cards.—Used by Magicians for performing Wonderful Tricks. Every boy a magician! Every man a conjurer! Every girl a witch! Every one astonished! They are the most superior Trick Cards ever offered fo sale, and with them you can perform some of the most remarkable illusions e* discovered. Mailed, with full directions, for 25 cents a pack.

The Black Art Fully Exposed and Laid Bare.—This book contains some of the most marvellous things in ancient and modern magic, jugglery, etc., ever printed, and has to be seen to be fully appreciated. Suffice it to say that any boy knowing the secrets it contains will be able to do things that will astonish all. Illustrated. Mailed for 25 cents.

Swimming and Skating.—A complete Guide for learners. Every reader should possess this book so as to learn how to swim. Many a young life has been nipped in the bud, many a home made desolate for the want of knowing how to swim. Very fully illustrated. Mailed for Twenty cents.

Singing Made Easy.—Explaining the pure Italian method of producing and cultivating the Voice, the Management of the Breath, the best way of Improving the Ear, and much valuable information, equally useful to professional singers and amateurs. Mailed for 20 cents.

The Amateur's Guide to Magic and Mystery.—An entirely new work, containing full and ample instructions on the Mysteries of Magic, Sleight-of-Hand Tricks, Card Tricks, etc The best work on Conjuring for Amateurs published. Illustrated. Mailed for 25 cents.

The American Sphinx.—A choice, curious and complete collection of Anagrams, Enigmas, Charades, Rebuses, Problems, Puzzles Cryptographs, Riddles, Conundrums, Decapitations, Word Changes, etc., etc. Profusely Illustrated. Mailed for 25 cents.

Life in the Back Woods.—A Guide to the Successful Hunting and Trapping of all kinds of Animals. This is at once the most complete and practical book now in the market. Mailed for 20 cents.

The Happy Home Songster.—A casket of time-honored vocal gems. Only favorite and world-wide known songs are admitted in this and following book. Mailed for 20 cents.

The Fireside Songster.—A collection of the best-known sentimental, humorous and comic songs. Mailed for 20 cents.

Address   **FRANK M. REED,**

139 Eighth Street, New York.

Courtship and Marriage; or, The Mysteries of Making Love fully Explained.

—This is an entirely new work on a most interesting subject. CONTENTS.—First steps in courtship; Advice to both parties at the outset; Introduction to the lady's family; Restrictions imposed by etiquette; What the lady should observe in early courtship; What the suitor should observe; Etiquette as to presents; The proposal; Mode of refusal when not approved; Conduct to be observed by a rejected suitor; Refusal by the lady's parents or guardians; Etiquette of an engagement; Demeanor of the betrothed pair; Should a courtship be long or short; Preliminary etiquette of a wedding; Fixing the day; How to be married; The trosseau; Duties to be attended to by the bridegroom; Who should be asked to the wedding; Duties of the bridesmaids and bridegroomsmen; Etiquette of a wedding; Costume of bride, bridesmaids, and bridegroom; Arrival at the church; The marriage ceremonial; Registry of the marriage; Return home, and wedding breakfast; Departure for the honeymoon; Wedding cards; Modern practice of "No Cards;" Reception and return of wedding visits; Practical advice to a newly married couple. Mailed for 15 cents.

How to Behave.

—A Hand-Book of Etiquette and Guide to True Politeness.—CONTENTS.—Etiquette and its uses; Introductions; Cutting acquaintances; Letters of introduction; Street etiquette; Domestic etiquette and duties; Visiting; Receiving company; Evening parties; The lady's toilet; The gentleman's toilet; Invitations: Etiquette of the ball-room; General rules of conversation; Bashfulness, and how to overcome it; Dinner parties; Table etiquette; Carving; Servants; Travelling; Visiting cards; Letter-writing; Conclusion. This is the best book of the kind yet published, and every person wishing to be considered well-bred, who wishes to understand the customs of good society, and to avoid incorrect and vulgar habits, should send for a copy. Mailed for 15 cents.

The Model Letter-Writer.

—A Comprehensive and Complete Guide and Assistant for those who desire to carry on epistolary correspondence—containing instructions for writing Letters of Introduction; Letters on Business; Letters of Recommendation; Applications for Employment; Letters of Congratulation; Letters of Condolence; Letters of Friendship and Relationship; Love Letters; Notes of Invitation; Letters of Favor, of Advice, and of Excuse, etc., etc., together with appropriate Answers to each. This is an invaluable book for those persons who have not had sufficient practice to enable them to write letters without great effort. Mailed for 15 cents.

The Complete Fortune-Teller and Dream Book.

—This book contains a complete Dictionary of Dreams, alphabetically arranged, with a clear interpretation of each dream, and the lucky numbers that belong to it. It includes Palmistry, or telling fortunes by the lines of the hand; fortune-telling by the grounds in a tea or coffee cup; how to read your future life by the white of an egg; tells how to know who your future husband will be, and how soon you will be married; fortune-telling by cards; Hymen's lottery; good and bad omens, etc., etc. Mailed for 15 cents.

The Lover's Companion.

—A book no lover should be without. It gives Handkerchief, Parasol, Glove and Fan Flirtations; also, Window and Dining-table Signalling; The Language of Flowers; How to kiss deliciously; Love Letters, and how to write them, with specimens; Bashfulness and Timidity, and how to overcome them, etc., etc. Mailed for 25 cents.

GOOD BOOKS FOR YOUNG AND OLD, MARRIED AND SINGLE.

CENTS.

Robinson Crusoe, profusely illustrated	30
The Shadow Pantomime—A miniature theatre for the little ones	30
How to Write Short-hand—Odell's System	25
The Art of Ventriloquism	15
Our Boys' and Girls' Favorite Speaker	20
Educating the Horse	25
Every Lady Her Own Dressmaker	20
Napoleon's Oraculum and Book of Fate	15
The Complete Guide to Swimming and Skating	20
The Happy Home Songster	20
The Fireside Songster	20
Singing Made Easy	20
Guide to Hunting and Trapping	20
The Black Art, Fully Exposed and Laid Bare	25
Magic Trick Cards	25
Amateur's Guide to Magic and Mystery	25
The American Sphinx	25
The Magic Dial	40
The Dancer's Guide and Ball-room Companion	25
Love and Courtship Cards	30
Leisure Hour Work for Ladies	20
How to Entertain a Social Party	25
How to Talk and Debate	15
The Model Letter-Writer	15
How to Behave	15
The Lover's Companion	25
Courtship and Marriage	15
How to Woo and How to Win	15
The Complete Fortune-Teller and Dream-Book	15
Old Secrets and New Discoveries	50
Laughing-Gas, with comic illustration	25
Salt, Pepper and Mustard—A book of fun	20
Health Hints	50
Preserving and Manufacturing Secrets	50
Secrets for Farmers	30
The Common-Sense Cook-Book	25
The Housewife's Treasure	30

☞ *If you have not one, send stamp for a catalogue.*

Address **FRANK M. REED,**
139 Eighth Street, New York.

A new book showing how to Acquire and Retain Bodily Symmetry, Health, Vigor, and Beauty. Its contents are as follows : Laws of Beauty—Air, Sunshine, Water, and Food—Work and Rest—Dress and Ornament—The Hair and its Management—Skin and Complexion—the Mouth—The Eyes, Ears and Nose—The Neck, Hands, and Feet—Growth and Marks that are Enemies of Beauty—Cosmetics and Perfumery.

Fat People.—It gives ample rules how Corpulency may be Cured—the Fat made Lean, Comely and Active.

Lean People.—It also gives directions, the following of which will enable Lean, Angular, Bony or Sharp Visaged People, to be Plump and Rosy Skinned.

Gray Hair.—It tells how Gray Hair may be Restored to its natural color without the aid of Dyes, Restorers, or Pomades.

Baldness.—It gives ample directions for Restoring Hair on Bald Heads, as well as how to stop Falling of the Hair, how to Curl the Hair, etc.

Beard and Mustache.—It tells what Young Men should do to acquire a Fine Silky and Handsome Beard and Mustache.

Freckles and Pimples.—It gives full directions for the Cure of Sunburn, Freckles, Pimples, Wrinkles, Warts, etc., so that they can be entirely removed.

Cosmetics.—This chapter, among other things, gives an Analysis of Perry's Moth and Freckle Lotion, Balm of White Lilies, Hagan's Magnolia Balm, Laird's Bloom of Youth, Phalon's Enamel, Clark's Restorative for the Hair, Chevalier's Life for the Hair, Ayer's Hair Vigor, Professor Wood's Hair Restorative, Hair Restorer America, Gray's Hair Restorative, Phalon's Vitalia, Ring's Vegetable Ambrosia, Mrs. Allen's World's Hair Restorer, Hall's Vegetable Sicilian Hair Renewer, Martha Washington Hair Restorative, etc., etc. (no room for more), showing how the lead, etc , in these mixtures cause disease and oftentimes premature death. Mailed for 50 cents.

The Management and Care of Infants and Children.—By Geo Combe, M.D. This is the best book ever written on the subject, and is one that no mother of a family can afford to be without   Its usual price in the book stores is $1.50, but it will be mailed—*the latest and most complete edition*—for only 75 cents.

Address   **FRANK M. REED,**

139 Eighth Street, New York.

OLD SECRETS AND NEW DISCOVERIES:

Containing Information of Rare Value for All Classes, in all Conditions of Society.

It tells all about *Electrical Psychology*, showing how you can biologize any person, and while under the influence he will do anything you may wish him, no matter how ridiculous it may be, and he cannot help doing it; also, how to *mesmerize*—a secret that has been sold over and over again for $10; how to make a person at a distance think of you, and how to charm those you meet and make them love you, whether they will or not.

It tells how to make the wonderful Magic or Invisible Photographs and Spirit Pictures; the Eggs of Pharo's Serpents, which when lighted, though but the size of a pea, there issues from it a coiling serpent; how to perform the Davenport Brothers' " Spirit Mysteries "; how to copy any kind of drawing or picture, and more wonderful still, to print pictures from the print itself; how to make gold and silver from block-tin (the least said about which, the better); also, how to take impressions from coins, and how to imitate gold and silver.

It tells how to make a horse appear as though he was badly foundered; to make a horse temporarily lame; how to make him stand by his food and not eat it; how to cure a horse from the crib or sucking wind; how to put a young countenance on the horse; how to cover up the heaves; how to make him appear as if he had the glanders; how to make a true-pulling horse baulk; how to nerve a horse that is lame, etc., etc. These horse secrets are being continually sold at one dollar each.

It tells how to make a cheap Galvanic Battery; how to plate and gild without a battery; how to make a candle burn all night; how to make a clock for 25 cents; how to detect counterfeit money; how to banish and prevent mosquitoes from biting; how to make yellow butter in winter; Circassian curling fluid; Sympathetic or Secret Writing Ink; Cologne Water; Artificial honey; Stammering; how to make large noses small; to cure drunkenness; to copy letters without a press; to obtain fresh blown flowers in winter; to make a good burning candle from lard; and scores of other wonderful things for which there is no room to mention. " *Old Secrets and New Discoveries* " is worth $5 to any person, but it will be mailed to any address on receipt of only 50 cents.

Address **FRANK M. REED,**

139 Eighth Street, New York.